Clean-Up Time!

Adapted by Patty Michaels

Based on the screenplays by Mary Jacobson
and Monique D. Hall

Poses and layouts by Jason Fruchter

Ready-to-Read

Simon Spotlight
New York   London   Toronto   Sydney   New Delhi

SIMON SPOTLIGHT
An imprint of Simon & Schuster Children's Publishing Division
1230 Avenue of the Americas, New York, New York 10020
This Simon Spotlight edition December 2020
© 2020 The Fred Rogers Company. All rights reserved.
All rights reserved, including the right of reproduction in whole or in part in any form.
SIMON SPOTLIGHT, READY-TO-READ, and colophon are registered trademarks of Simon & Schuster, Inc.
For information about special discounts for bulk purchases, please contact Simon & Schuster
Special Sales at 1-866-506-1949 or business@simonandschuster.com.
Manufactured in the United States of America 1020 LAK
2 4 6 8 10 9 7 5 3 1
ISBN 978-1-5344-7987-6 (hc)
ISBN 978-1-5344-7986-9 (pbk)
ISBN 978-1-5344-7988-3 (eBook)

Hi, neighbor!
Today Katerina and I
are going on a picnic.

We are going
to have our picnic
at the playground!

We ride Trolley
to the playground.

My mom and dad come with us.

Oh no!
The playground is
covered with garbage!

Dad says the wind
must have caused
the mess.

King Friday goes to the playground. He asks everyone to help clean up.

It is important to keep our neighborhood clean.

We each get a pair
of gloves and bags
to put the garbage in.

We can play after we clean up the playground.

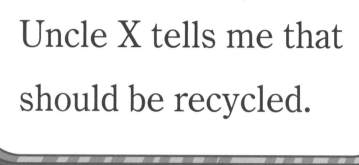

Uncle X tells me that should be recycled.

To recycle means to turn something old into something new!

Then O the Owl shows me a book about how to recycle.

Katerina does not want
to help clean up.
She wants to play.

I tell her we cannot play because the playground is still messy.

When we all clean together, we can make a big difference in our neighborhood!

Miss Elaina comes over to help us.

O the Owl

keeps on recycling.

We do a great job cleaning up together!

Now we can all enjoy a picnic at the playground.

Then it is time to play!